SEED

EVERYTHING FOR JESUS
DEVOTIONALS FOR A MONTH

BRO. SUNIL BINKAM

Preface

Dear Child of God,

Welcome to "Seeds," a collection of devotionals for a month. Over the next 31 days, you will embark on a spiritual journey rooted in the biblical metaphor of the seed. Each devotional is designed to help you explore different aspects of your faith, drawing parallels between the growth of a seed and the development of your spiritual life.

This book was inspired by a deep desire to see believers grow in their relationship with God. Through these devotionals, I aim to provide practical insights and spiritual nourishment, encouraging you to cultivate a deeper connection with the Lord.

From understanding the significance of small beginnings to recognizing the importance of maintaining fertile ground for spiritual growth, each day's message is a step toward a more fruitful and fulfilling spiritual life. We will explore topics such as faith, righteousness, and the obstacles that can hinder our growth, always returning to the central theme of God's unending grace and provision.

As you meditate on these devotionals, I pray that you find encouragement, inspiration, and a renewed sense of purpose in your walk with God. May these seeds of faith take root in your heart, grow, and bear abundant fruit in your life. Thank you for joining me on this journey. May God bless you richly as you seek to grow in Him.

In Christ,
Bro. Sunil Binkam

Dedication and Thanks

Dedication

This book is dedicated to my Lord and Savior, Jesus Christ. Without His grace and love, this journey would not have been possible. All glory and honor belong to Him.

Thanks

My sincere thanks to the Holy Spirit of God, who helped me receive and recognize the revelation and the guidance of God while compiling these devotionals.

I would like to express my deepest gratitude to my Pastor, Bro. S. Raj Kamal of Jesus Cares You Ministries, for his unwavering prayers and encouragement. His spiritual guidance has been instrumental in nurturing my desire to do something meaningful for the Lord. Thank you for your continual support and faith in my journey.

Visit https://jesuscaresyou.in to know more about his ministry

About the Author

Bro. Sunil Binkam is a devoted follower of Jesus Christ, chosen to be saved, born again, and to broadcast the truths of God's word to the world. Responding to God's calling, he established an online presence through his YouTube channel "https://youtube.com/@efjsocial" and his website "https://efj.org.in". By profession, he is a software engineer, but by passion, he is a worker of the Lord.

Bro. Sunil has served as a youth leader, preacher, songwriter, and content creator by God's grace. In November 2023, God inspired him to compile daily devotionals with 12 themes, motivating him to publish these as monthly devotionals. He believes this approach aligns with God's greater purpose over traditional yearly devotionals.

This book is the first in the theme-based monthly devotional series called, "Everything For Jesus: Devotionals for a Month."

He seeks prayer support to continue faithfully serving the Lord according to his God-given capacity.

INDEX

INDEX

DAY 1 - WHAT SEEDS YOU HAVE?

A sower went out to sow his seed … Luke 8:5

The term "sow" means to scatter seeds for growth, introduce into a suitable environment, or set in motion. Similarly, "seed" refers to grains, a source of development, or a unit of reproduction.

A seed is anything invested to produce results. For spiritual growth, we need to sow spiritual seeds. But to sow, we must possess seeds. What seeds do we have to sow?

Time: Time can be invested or sown to reap fruits based on how it is spent. For example, investing time in meditating on God's word will yield knowledge about God.

Money: Money can be invested in God's work, reaping rewards for contributing to the progress of the kingdom of heaven.

Talents: Our talents, when invested in the work of God, yield rewards for being part of the kingdom of heaven.

Today's focus is the seed you have for God. On this New Year's Day, take time to understand your seed. Sharing the word of God on social media can encourage at least one person, bringing goodness in His sight. Praying for a neighbor's salvation or problems, helping your church's needs, and investing time to align with God's word in one area of your life are seeds. Discover what you have today and use it for God's glory.

Let's Pray

Gracious heavenly Father, thank You for guiding us on the concept of seed. Help me identify my seeds and grant me the wisdom to use them for Your glory. In the precious name of our Lord and Savior Jesus Christ, we pray. Amen.

DAY 2 - SEED NEEDS TIME TO GROW

As soon as it was sprung up… Luke 8:6

The term "spring up" means to come into existence suddenly. When a seed is sown, there won't be immediate outward growth or evidence of it. However, beneath the surface, roots start to pierce into the ground. This principle applies to spiritual seeds as well.

When we sow our time, money, resources, energy, and talents into spiritual matters, the result is not immediate. Similarly, when the word of God is sown in our hearts through personal meditation or church services, the result is not immediate. Understanding this truth is crucial to standing strong even when we don't see visible changes in our life despite practicing spiritual discipline.

Patience is essential in the growth process, both in the natural world and in our spiritual lives. Just as a farmer waits patiently for the crop to grow after sowing the seed, we must also wait for the spiritual fruits to manifest. Trust that God is at work beneath the surface, nurturing and preparing us for the right season of growth and harvest.

Let's Pray

Heavenly Father, thank You for teaching us the importance of patience and trust in Your timing. Help me to understand that growth takes time and to remain faithful even when I do not see immediate results. May I continue to sow my seeds diligently, trusting that You are at work in my life. In Jesus' name, Amen.

DAY 3 - ARE YOU SOWING ON THE WAYSIDE

and as he sowed, some fell by the way side; and it was trodden down - Luke 8:5

Wayside means on the edge of the road. When a person sows his seeds in a field, he will scatter them by throwing. Some seeds may fall on the edge of the road instead of field.

Here field is the right and intended place. But roadside is not the right place to sow. If we imagine a worker who sows these seeds, he will know the boundary of his owner's field and he should know where to sow.

In the same way, we belong to our heavenly Father. He knows the boundaries of everything in our life. He is the one who gives the seed to sow whether it is time, money or opportunity etc. But when we don't invest them according to the will of God, we are actually making them to fall on the wayside.

If you remember Saul, God gave him the words of instructions to exterminate Amalekites. But Saul did not do according to the word. This is an example of wayside experience. In our life also, we must be careful not to do anything against the will of God to get good fruit out of our life.

Let's Pray

Dear Loving heavenly Father, thank you for teaching me today about the wayward sowing. Help me not to invest anything outside of your will. Give me your wisdom and grace to understand your will. I pray in the name of Jesus Christ Amen.

DAY 4 - YOUR SEEDS HAVE LIFE

…and it was trodden down, and the fowls of the air devoured it – Luke 8:5

There are two activities mentioned in the above verse: trodden down and devoured. In the context and based on the explanation given by Jesus in later verses, it refers to Satan stealing away the word planted in our hearts.

But why is Satan interested in stealing the seeds? As we have already learned, a seed can be anything that starts small but grows to be fruitful. Particularly at the beginning of the new year, we will have many resolutions. Most of the time they will just be shelved. We may want to change a bad habit or live a more godly way than last year. But after a couple of days, many distractions wage war against our minds, and we will eventually lose track.

Today we are not going to look at the reasons for these failures, but we want to focus on one truth: our seeds have life in them. When you want to change some aspect for the sake of God, it has life in it. If that life is nurtured with a fertile heart, the life of that seed will be manifested, and you will see the fruit in your life. That is the reason Satan always tries to steal the efforts when they are still like seeds.

Will you just stop today and realize the life in your small decision you made to change for God? Thank Him for giving you the opportunity to sow it. Pray to Him to give you the courage and wisdom to nurture it.

Remember, the seeds, which are your small decisions to change for God, are valuable in the sight of God. That's why Satan is interested in stealing away those valuable seeds.

Let's Pray

Dear heavenly Father, thank you for reminding me about the life in my small decisions to change and align to your will. Thank you for reminding me how valuable they are and help me to gaurd them with your help abd wisdom. In the name of Jesus I pray, Amen

DAY 5 - KNOW YOUR GROUND BEFORE YOU SOW

A sower went out to sow his seed – Luke 8:5

The seeds are designated to be sown in a field that is prepared. The field is outside his house, and he needs to prepare it before he even sows them.

The time, money, talents, and resources we want to utilize for the glory of God are our seeds. Before sowing them, which means using them, we need to know where the field is. A sower cannot sow his seeds in any field but in his owner's field only.

Our owner is the heavenly Father. The details of the field given for us to sow these seeds are revealed through His son Jesus Christ via the word of God and the Holy Spirit.

We must wait in prayer to understand where we should invest our time, money, talents, and resources, and then we can go out and use them for the glorious purposes of God.

In our practical life, consider how we might feel called to volunteer our time. Instead of randomly choosing activities, we should pray for guidance to find where God wants us to serve. For example, someone might feel a calling to mentor young people. By praying and seeking God's direction, they can find the right organization or group where their efforts will be most fruitful.
Today's reflection is to understand your designated field or ground. Then, prayerfully start using your seeds for the glory of God.

Let's Pray

Lord, guide me to understand and recognize my designated field. Help me to prayerfully invest my time, money, talents, and resources in ways that glorify You. In Jesus' name, Amen.

DAY 6 - DOES YOUR GROUND HAVE MOISTURE?

And some fell upon a rock; and as soon as it was sprung up, it withered away, because it lacked moisture – Luke 8:6

In this verse, it talks about rock. But where is this rock? In the field only. When the sower went out to sow his seeds, he did not prepare all the ground. There is a part in the ground where rocks are there. These seeds fell on that rocky ground. The important thing is the seeds which fell on the good ground and the rocky ground both sprung up. But when time passed, the plants sprung up from the rocky ground withered.

This is a very apt analogy for our spiritual life. When we hear the word of God, we will be motivated and will start acting on it someway or other. Couple of days it will be nice and happy. But afterwards we will lack interest or focus and whatever we started will just eventually be stopped.

I have personal experience in prayer discipline, family prayers and keeping myself away from worldly entertainment etc. Most of the times I took some measures to follow the decision and discipline. But eventually could not stand strong for it. The rocky ground lacks moisture. Moisture refers to the unwavering zeal. This zeal is required to stand strong for the decisions we took. Let's ask God's help to keep the zeal in our hearts alive.

Let's Pray

Lord, help me to identify and remove the rocks in my life. Guide me to maintain unwavering zeal for Your word and strengthen my commitment. In Jesus' name, Amen.

And some fell among thorns; and the thorns sprang up with it, and choked it. -Luke 8:7

In this verse, we see a different ground where thorny bushes choke the growth of plants. Unlike rocky soil, which prevents moisture, thorny bushes hinder plant growth, preventing them from bearing fruit.

Thorns represent worldly pleasures. While we may have zeal for God's work and start well, indulging in worldly pleasures can gradually take over our spiritual efforts, leading to unfruitfulness.

I remember how my zeal for God's work led me to start my YouTube channel. Initially, I posted regular content and prayed for people. However, as I spent more time on lesser priority things, my efforts did not yield results.

To address this, we must remove the thorny bushes and use fertilizers. The word of God, as a sword, helps remove thorns and, as spiritual food, renews our passion and zeal, enabling us to flourish.

Let's examine ourselves, confess before God, and remove the thorns in our lives.

Let's Pray

Lord, help me to identify and remove the thorns in my life. Guide me to prioritize Your word and grow in faith. In Jesus' name, Amen.

Also when I cry and shout, he shutteth out my prayer – Lamentations 3:8

In this verse, we see that God doesn't listen to our prayers even if we cry out loud when our relationship with Him is spoiled. Praying is like sowing, and the prayer itself is the seed. The answer is the fruit, and the ground is our relationship with God. Previous chapters show that the people's relationship with God was broken, leading to His anger and wrath.

Similarly, in our lives, we often kindle God's anger by disobeying His word, living compromised lives, and losing zeal for Him. This creates rocky or thorny ground.

Today, we live under God's manifested grace through Jesus Christ. His word is near, and through Jesus' sacrifice, we can confess our shortcomings and receive cleansing. God is faithful to cleanse us from all filth and uncleanness (1 John 1:9).

Even in Lamentations, it is written about God's grace and mercies, which are new every morning (Lamentations 3:22-23).

Let us set our relationship with God right and prepare our ground by removing stones and thorny bushes, so we can receive answers to our prayers and enjoy God's guidance and provision.

Let's Pray

Heavenly Father, thank You for the gift of prayer. Help me to see my prayers as seeds that can bring forth Your blessings and purposes in my life. Strengthen my faith and persistence as I seek Your will. May my prayers bear fruit for Your glory. In Jesus' name, Amen.

And other fell on good ground, and sprang up, and bare fruit an hundredfold – Luke 8:8

In the natural physical ground, stones, rocks, thorny bushes, and weeds naturally appear without any effort. An unattended ground naturally has these obstacles. Similarly, in our lives, if we do not work on ourselves, we become occupied with fleshly and worldly desires.

A good ground means a ground free of stones, rocks, thorny bushes, or weeds that hinder seed growth. Naturally, this isn't possible; hence, good grounds are made. Isaiah 5:2 states: "And he fenced it, and gathered out the stones thereof, and planted it with the choicest vine." The ground was prepared by removing stones and protecting it, making it good ground.

We can equate many things in our lives to ground, like our mind or areas of interest. But on a higher level, the ultimate good ground is our relationship with the heavenly Father through Jesus Christ and the fellowship of the Holy Spirit. This relationship doesn't come naturally but requires deliberate effort and decision. By consulting the Father through the word and prayer, our relationship grows, and our life becomes good ground.

Shall we make a deliberate decision today to cultivate a relationship with the heavenly Father? It requires faith in Jesus' finished work on the cross and belief that we aren't bound by our failures. It needs faith in the Holy Spirit's constant presence and the realization that the heavenly Father paid the price to transform our natural state of failure.

Let's Pray

Lord, help me to cultivate a relationship with You and transform my life into good ground. Guide me to remove obstacles and grow in faith. In Jesus' name, Amen.

DAY 10 - THE SEED MUST FALL ON THE GROUND

And they say unto him, We have here but five loaves, and two fishes – Matthew 14:17

Today's meditation is a little deeper. God explains the principle of sowing seeds through this passage.

Today's verse is well known. It is from the context of feeding 5 loaves of bread and two small fishes to more than 5000 people. If we allow the Holy Spirit to work in us, we can observe a few important points.

1. **Seeds**: Seeds are the smallest unit of reproduction. The 5 loaves of bread and 2 small fishes are like seeds. They are very little in quantity.
2. **Ground**: Seeds are placed in prepared ground so that the work of growth begins. Here, Jesus' call to feed is the ground. When the small boy and disciples submitted to the call, they sowed the seeds into the ground.
3. **Fruit**: The results we await from the seeds sown. Here, the loaves and fishes multiplied. The seed's growth depends on the nutrients it can get from the ground. We learn that Jesus' call to feed is the ground, providing necessary things for them to grow.

This illustrates an important principle related to sowing seeds that we can practice in our lives. When we submit to God's calling, He provides the necessary support and environment to establish and grow in the calling.

May God help us to recognize His calling, submit our small beginnings as seeds sown into good ground, witness, and testify to the supernatural growth in our life, and fulfill the purpose of our calling.

Let's Pray

Dear heavenly Father, thank you for teaching the wonderful revelation about seeding. Help me to faithfully sow my small beginnings towards your calling. Now I knew these small beginnings one day would grow to fulfill your will and satisfy many, I thank you and pray in the name of my Lord and Saviour Jesus Christ, Amen!

DAY 11 - THE OUTER SHELL MUST BREAK

Except a corn of wheat fall into the ground and die, it abideth alone: but if it die, it bringeth forth much fruit – John 12:24

This verse highlights that for a seed to grow, its outer shell must break. The seed of wheat, after falling on the ground, has its outer shell destroyed, allowing new life to spring up.

In our practical life, consider the example of investing time in the meditation of the word. Our seed is the time, and the ground is the word. Initially, we may face challenges like inability to understand or demotivation. But as we consistently meditate, the word works to break these barriers, and life springs up from the word.

Similarly, in changing a bad habit, our small beginnings of change are wrapped with failures and stress, and the ground is the word of God. As our efforts are nurtured in the word, the outer shell of failures and stress breaks, and new, good habits emerge.

We recognize that the outer shell, representing lack of faith, failures, or demotivation, must break for new life to manifest. Consistent nurturing in the word of God facilitates this transformation, leading to success and flourishing.

Let's Pray

Lord, help me to break away from my old self and fully surrender to Your will. Guide me through the process of transformation and renewal, so that I may produce abundant spiritual fruit. In Jesus' name, Amen.

DAY 12 - IDENTIFY TARES AMONG THE WHEAT

But while men slept, his enemy came and sowed tares among the wheat, and went his way – Matthew 13:25

The wheat and tares look alike when they are small, but at harvest time, the difference is clear.

People sow good seeds with good intentions, but the enemy sows bad ones to cause loss.

Jesus explains that, as His followers, we aim to align with God's word. This is a genuine thought for every believer when they hear the word and start applying it to their lives.

However, during this time, the devil brings distractions to hinder growth.

For example, we might decide to improve an area of our life but get distracted by other issues, delaying our progress. The wheat represents the importance of following God's word, while the tares symbolize distractions. Both seem important initially, but the results reveal the true value.

Tares do not destroy the yield but reduce it, consuming valuable resources. Similarly, our initial decisions to change take longer when we indulge in unnecessary activities, wasting time and energy.

Jesus explains that there is an appointed time to distinguish what is important. On that day, we can decide to discard the tares. May that day come soon.

Let's Pray

Dear Heavenly Father, thank You for teaching me another aspect through the lessons of the seed. Help me to understand the right things in my life to give importance to, and glorify Your name. Help me to identify the tares in my life early and prepare consciously to separate them at the appointed time. I pray in the name of Jesus, Amen!

DAY 13 - YOUR ASPIRATION NEEDS ZEAL TO BECOME AN ACCOMPLISHMENT

And when the sun was up, they were scorched; and because they had no root, they withered away. -Matthew 13:6

In this verse, we see the condition of a seed that has grown into a plant. It has grown on rocky ground where moisture is not present. When the sun became hot, it withered because it had no root.

If we observe this condition, the ground was rocky. The seed became a plant, but during difficult times, it could not withstand because it lacked roots. The roots could not get the essence of the ground because of the rocks. The plant desired to survive but had no root connection with the ground, which had water and nutrients for it to survive in tough conditions.

The root has two main purposes: to get water and nutrients for the plant and to give the plant grip to stand. For believers, the word of God is the ground. The rocks on the ground, as we learned previously, represent the lack of zeal. The roots represent the desire or aspirations. Even if the plant has roots, if they cannot penetrate the ground, they cannot stand and survive. Similarly, if the ground is good but the seed does not sprout and no roots come out, there will be no growth.

For our spiritual growth in the Word of God, fellowship with the Holy Spirit, and effective pursuit of the revealed purposes of God, as well as for success in our daily personal needs and careers, we require two crucial ingredients: the desire or aspiration and the zeal to fuel that aspiration into accomplishment. May God help us to have both the desire and zeal to stand strong and grow strong for His glory.

Let's Pray

Dear loving Heavenly Father, thank You for teaching me today about the important aspects of growth. I confess that most of the time, I lack the zeal. I fail to turn my desires into accomplishments. Help me in this area and renew my zeal to live for You. Help me to take the first steps toward kindling the zeal in me. I pray in the name of my Lord and Savior, Jesus Christ. Amen.

DAY 14 - PLOUGH YOUR GROUND

And some fell among thorns; and the thorns sprung up, and choked them – Matthew 13:7

If we carefully observe this verse, when the seeds were sown, there were only insignificant thorns. But as the seeds grew, these thorns also grew, eventually outgrowing the plants, preventing them from bearing fruit.

This teaches us that every new year or when God's word speaks to us, we take initiatives to set things right and make small beginnings. However, worldly desires and pleasures, initially insignificant, can grow and take priority, hindering our resolutions. These unhealthy desires overpower our zeal, stopping our spiritual growth.Before sowing seeds, the ground must be prepared, removing stones and weeds. For our lives, the word of God acts as the plough:

The word of God is quick, and powerful, and sharper than any two-edged sword - Hebrews 4:12

It's crucial to pray and seek God's guidance to identify obstacles before starting any work for Him. God, as our loving Father, hears, sees, and understands our situations.

Even if you fail today in changing your life for God's glory, don't be discouraged. Return to the word, ask God in prayer, and He will guide you. God can speak to you through meditation, church services, prayer meetings, or even messages on YouTube or WhatsApp. He loves us and died to give us life. Let's get back to the Father, and with the help of the word, prepare our ground to make the sown seeds fruitful.

Let's Pray

Dear loving Heavenly Father, thank You for teaching me an important aspect of the growth of a seed. In my life, there are many thorns that have outgrown my desire for You. Thank You for reminding me once more that Your word is waiting for me to use it to plough my heart. You are always waiting for me without abandoning me. Thank You for Your love, dear Father. I thank You and submit my prayer in the name of my Lord and Savior, Jesus Christ. Amen!

DAY 15 - UNINTENDED PLANTS WILL BE UPROOTED

Every plant that my heavenly Father has not planted will be uprooted" – Matthew 15:13

Through our daily meditation on the concept of the "seed," we understand that everything we begin, no matter how small, is like a seed. Every desire to do good comes from the Father's inspiration, while anything not aligned with goodness stems from the enemy. The verse speaks of a "plant," signifying the growth from seed to plant.

This teaches us a crucial aspect of life. When seeking spiritual or worldly growth in alignment with God's word, we often initiate processes that progress from a seed state to a plant state. Before these endeavors become significant, our Father, who is both our parent and owner, may uproot the plants that didn't originate from the seeds He planted.

For instance, if we feel called to work for God's kingdom and join others in preaching the gospel, it may seem promising. However, if God has a different plan, He may allow setbacks and lead us away from that path. It might result in a period of isolation, similar to Elijah before the drought. Yet, during this time, God has a miraculous plan for us.

People or desires that don't align with our true calling will eventually be removed by God. Anything hindering our growth according to His will is eliminated because of His love. It's akin to a parent immediately taking away dangerous objects from a child. Though the child may not perceive the danger, the parent knows what is best for their well-being.

Let's Pray

Dear heavenly Father, I thank you for today's lesson. I now understand that not everything in my life is inherently good, especially if it opposes the purpose You've ordained for me. Help me recognize these situations, trust Your guidance, and remain consistently under Your divine leading. I pray in the name of our Lord and Savior, Jesus Christ. Amen.

DAY 16 - GOOD SEEDS COMES FROM GOOD FRUIT

For every tree is known by his own fruit – Luke 6:43,44

Whether a tree is good or not is known by its fruit. That means until a tree bears fruit, we cannot decide whether it is a good tree or a bad tree. More specifically, unless someone experiences the fruits, we can't determine if a tree is good or not.

When multiple people experience the fruit of the tree, a stronger conclusion is made, and it is declared that the tree is not good. Based on this experience, no one will gather the seeds of such trees. If anyone sees someone planting these seeds, they will immediately warn them about its fruit.

This is an important spiritual lesson. Our parents, well-wishers, and spiritual forerunners tell us by their experience not to get involved in certain things. It is better not to get involved in those things. Expecting a good result from something that others have warned against is impossible.

For example, parents and well-wishers advise young people not to associate with friends who drink, tease others, and gamble. They say that if you associate with them, your life will be spoiled. If a young person disregards this advice and gets involved, they cannot expect a great life.

So, based on the word of God, through His servants and various channels, whatever God has told us is not good, let us refrain from indulging in it. We cannot expect good fruit if we willingly make an obviously wrong choice according to His word.

Let's Pray

Dear Loving heavenly Father, thank you for teaching me today about the good and bad trees being identified by their fruit. Help me to refrain from involving in any bad things. Help me to root out already planted ones. I pray in the name of my Lord and Saviour Jesus Christ, Amen!

DAY 17 - NEW BLESSINGS ARE SPRINGING UP

Behold, I will do a new thing; now it shall spring forth – Isaiah 43:19

God, in His infinite wisdom, uses the phrase "I will do," signifying that the transformation He has in store is not yet present in our lives. The anticipation builds as He declares, "now it will spring forth."

Imagine a seed lying beneath the surface, ready to burst forth into life. This imagery conveys God's work in our lives. As God addresses us, we find that the ground where this seed is sown is the soil of our lives.

As we've learned, in any kind of ground, the seed will sprout, whether rocky, thorny, or fertile. However, a crucial question remains – will it grow and bear fruit? God, in His divine role, has done His part, sowing the seed of new blessings. He assures us that it will spring up; evidence of His work will manifest in our lives. Yet, for this blessing to flourish into a fruitful tree, our role is vital. We must prepare the ground, maintaining it with spiritual nourishment and diligence.

Despite the blessings bestowed upon the Israelites, their failure to uphold a righteous lifestyle prevented them from fully enjoying God's gifts. Their journey reminds us to examine our own lives and ensure we are ready to embrace and sustain the blessings destined for us by God.

Today, God extends His hand with a new blessing. The question is: Are you ready to receive it? Are you prepared to allow His work to unfold in your life? Let us examine our hearts, clear away the stumbling blocks, and embrace the new thing God desires to bring forth.

Let's Pray

Dear Loving heavenly Father, I recognize Your readiness to shower me with the best blessings. However, I confess that I have not always been prepared to align with Your blessings. Empower me to be steadfast in faith, to fully embrace the new blessings You have prepared for me. Grant me the wisdom to align my thoughts, actions, and desires with Your will. I pray in the name of my Lord and Saviour Jesus Christ, Amen!

DAY 18 - SOW IN THE SPIRITUAL TO REAP IN THE PHYSICAL

But seek ye first the kingdom of God, and his righteousness; and all these things shall be added unto you – Mathew 6:33

If we meditate on Matthew 6:25-34, we understand that Jesus discusses how birds and flowers are provided for by God. Birds do not sow, yet they are fed. Flowers do not weave, yet they are beautifully clothed. But for us, we sow seeds and make clothes with wisdom given by God. Today, we focus on "seek ye first the kingdom of God, and his righteousness; and all these things shall be added unto you."

When God says "all these things," He means our basic needs like food, drink, and clothing (Matthew 6:31). God ensures these needs are met. If these necessities are the fruit, then the seed we must sow is "seeking the kingdom of God and his righteousness."

Good seed brings good fruit. When we desire to understand God's will and ways, we yearn to understand His kingdom. As God said, "Seek, and you shall find" – Matthew 7:7. The desire to know God is the seed we plant in the Word of God. Without zeal, it's like lacking moisture in rocky ground. Difficult subjects or false interpretations are like thorny bushes, hindering the Word's growth.

However, if we maintain fellowship with the Holy Spirit and let Him teach us, our hearts become fertile ground. The Word will manifest in our lives, yielding 30-fold, 60-fold, and 100-fold fruit. According to Matthew 6:33, when we seek the heavenly, earthly blessings are added. If we sow in the spiritual realm, guided by the Holy Spirit, we will reap in the physical realm.

Let's Pray

Dear loving heavenly Father, thank you for teaching me today about the aspect of sowing in the spiritual realm and reaping in the physical realm. Lord, help me to practice this in my life. Help me to trust your word and the guidance of the Holy Spirit and build my life as a testimony in the physical realm. I pray in the name of my Lord and Saviour Jesus Christ, Amen!

DAY 19 - CAN GOD CORRUPT THE SEED?

Behold, I will corrupt your seed -Malachi 2:3

Now he that ministereth seed to the sower both minister bread for your food, and multiply your seed sown, and increase the fruits of your righteousness - 2 Corinthians 9:10

Yes, it is God Himself who gives the seed, and when it is sown, He multiplies it. But in today's verse from Malachi, we see that God Himself says He will corrupt the seed. If the one who blesses our seed to be fruitful says He will corrupt the seed, who else can help us? It is an utterly dire situation.

But why did this situation arise? "If ye will not hear, and if ye will not lay it to heart, to give glory unto my name, saith the LORD of hosts, I will even send a curse upon you, and I will curse your blessings: yea, I have cursed them already, because ye do not lay it to heart." - Malachi 2:2

Here, God accuses us of not being mindful of glorifying His name through our lives. Our life encompasses everything that we talk, walk, do, and think. Many times we pray in our troubles and distress, and God delivers us as a loving Father. Then we forget Him and continue in our own ways. We are interested in receiving the blessings but forget that a blessing is like a seed. It needs to be planted in a well-prepared ground, which is our life, mindful of the glory of God. Then the blessings will be fruitful, and we can enjoy them in our lives.

Today, God reminds us to turn back to Him and cleanse everything that comes against the glory of our Lord in our lives.

Let's Pray

Dear Heavenly Father, thank You for Your wonderful admonition. You do not want us to perish but to set our lives right and enjoy abundantly fruitful blessings by aligning our lives to Your word. Help us to heed Your word and set things right in our lives. We pray in the name of our Lord and Savior, Jesus Christ. Amen!

DAY 20 - WHO GIVES YOU THE SEED?

he that ministereth seed to the sower – 2 Corinthians 9:10

If we consider a physical field, when the farmer prepares for the season, he buys the seeds to sow in his fields. He goes to the source, pays for the seeds, and brings them back.

In our physical and spiritual lives, our life is the ground, and the seeds must be bought. We have two sources: our loving Heavenly Father and Satan. The Heavenly Father has seeds that bring satisfaction, grace, and glory. Satan's seeds lead to rebellion, addiction, and bondage.

Today marks the beginning of the season. If you want to reap joy, happiness, and the fullness of God's glory, ask, seek, and knock at God's door. If you are lazy, Satan will take the opportunity to deceive you and trap you.

Some examples of seeds we can ask God for are:
1. **Clarity of Calling:** When you ask God for clarity of your calling, He provides the seed, nurtures it, and ensures you act according to your calling.
2. **Breakthrough in Career**: A breakthrough is like a seed. It is a small turning point that significantly impacts your life.
3. **Marriage and Family Establishment**: Marriage is precious. Many rush into relationships without waiting on God. If we wait, He will open the door to the best companion and bless the marriage with happiness and joy.

We can apply this to any area of life: career, relationships, money, ministry, etc. God gives the right and best seeds we could ever imagine. May the Lord help us to seek Him for the seeds from now on.

Let's Pray

Dear Loving heavenly Father, thank you for reminding me about the source of seeds. I confess that multiple times, I allowed the seeds of the enemy, to be sown in my life. But indeed my life belongs to you and you have the best seed for my life. Help me Lord to only receive the seeds from you in every situation. I pray in the name of Jesus, Amen!

He … multiply your seed sown, and increase the fruits – 2 Corinthians 9:10

Sowing seeds is not enough to reap fruit; it's just the beginning. Many factors must be managed. The climate should support growth, and birds and rats might try to destroy your seeds. Tender care is required from sowing to harvesting.

Similarly, when we start small, it's just the beginning. We may face opposition, discouraging situations, and slow progress. But remember this truth: "It is God who multiplies the seed sown." Sowing and nurturing with water and fertilizers is a law God established. Similarly, God has set spiritual principles for our lives. If we follow them, growth will occur.

Psalm 1 is a principle. We need to carefully choose where we walk, stand, and sit. If we position ourselves near the abundant supply of God's word and the Holy Spirit, we will be fruitful in all seasons, whether good or bad.

Today, God reminds us that He makes the seed develop, grow, and become abundantly fruitful. We need to be planted near His continuous supply of water, which is His word and Spirit.

Let's Pray

Dear loving heavenly Father thank you for teaching today about another important principle of being planted where the water supply is abundant. Help me to build my life with your word and the revelation from that word through Holy Spirit. I pray in the name of Jesus Christ, Amen!

DAY 22 - GOD SOWS RIGHTEOUSNESS AND WE WILL REAP SALVATION

let the earth open, and let them bring forth salvation, and let righteousness spring up together – Isaiah 45:8

In this verse, God compares salvation to fruit and righteousness to the seed that springs up from the earth. We understand from this verse that righteousness comes first, grows, and brings forth salvation.

Remember God's words to Abraham about Sodom and Gomorrah: "And the LORD said, If I find in Sodom fifty righteous within the city, then I will spare all the place for their sakes." - Genesis 18:26. God searched for righteousness in the city but did not find it, so there was no salvation for Sodom and Gomorrah.

What about us? We are all sinners falling short of God's glory. But our gracious God has sown in us the seed of righteousness through Jesus Christ's sacrifice. "Even the righteousness of God which is by faith of Jesus Christ unto all and upon all them that believe" - Romans 3:22. Righteousness by faith in Jesus is like a seed planted in our lives by God. The fruit it brings is salvation. This seed needs care, removing rocks and thistles. Thus, we read:

"Work out your own salvation with fear and trembling." - Philippians 2:12. This means working to reap the fruit of our righteousness. How do we do this? "But thou, O man of God, flee these things; and follow after righteousness, godliness, faith, love, patience, meekness. " -1 Timothy 6:11-12

Our loving God, through Jesus, has given us righteousness by faith. We need to keep it safe until we reap the fruit of salvation. Praise be to God.

Let's Pray

Dear loving heavenly Father, thank you for teaching today about the righteousness being a seed and the salvation being the fruit. Because I cannot produce righteousness works by my own, you gave me righteousness as a free gift by the faith in Jesus Christ and kept your Holy Spirit within me to lead me and guide me to nurture the righteousness to produce the salvation. I thank you with my whole heart. I pray in the name of Jesus Christ, Amen.

DAY 23 - REMOVE THE THORNS OF ADULTERY FROM YOUR LIFE

When I would have healed... then the iniquity of Ephraim was discovered. They are all adulterers – Hosea 7:1,4,8

"When I would have healed…" indicates that healing was supposed to happen but didn't because of Ephraim's iniquity. This prevented the healing God intended.
Just as seeds in thorny ground are choked, God's plan for Israel's healing was obstructed. Healing means making whole and perfect, which God wanted for Israel.

In our lives, God has many perfect plans. He wants us to achieve perfection that we cannot attain without Him. However, there are thorns in our lives obstructing our journey to perfection. One aspect discussed is "adulterers," referring to unfaithfulness, like a spouse being dishonest in a marriage, which leads to an unholy relationship.

God's heart is shown in Hosea 7:10-16, where God was willing to lead, guide, strengthen, and love them, but they sought help from other people and kings instead of God. Despite experiencing God's help multiple times, they turned to powerful men instead of God. This is why God uses the term "adulterers."

If we remove these thorny bushes, growth will be good, and we can enjoy the fruit. God can tolerate many things but not His children seeking help elsewhere when He is always ready to help.

In our current time, advanced science and technology lead people to question God, preventing dependence on His guidance and leading to spiritual stagnation, like thorny bushes overcoming good plants.

Let's Pray

Dear Loving Heavenly Father, thank You for loving us. Thank You for Your desire to lead and guide us. You are the Creator, Miracle Worker, all-knowing, and all-powerful God, and You want to lead us to perfection. Thank You for Your love. Help us remove the heart of an adulterer and give us the heart of a loyal spouse. I pray in the name of our Lord and Savior, Jesus Christ. Amen.

DAY 24 - WATERING ENABLES HEALTHY GROWTH

I have planted, Apollos watered; but God gave the increase – 1 Corinthians 3:6

Today, we observe another aspect in the growth of a seed: "watering." Watering a plant from the seed stage is crucial. Water facilitates food preparation and the transportation of nutrients required by various parts of the plant. Spiritually, watering represents nourishing with the word of God, as articulated in Proverbs:

"My son, attend unto my wisdom, and bow thine ear to my understanding: That thou mayest regard discretion, and that thy lips may keep knowledge." – Proverbs 5:1-2

God's wisdom and understanding come through His word. By paying attention and listening to the word of God, we gradually strengthen ourselves and can make righteous choices in various situations. In this manner, we grow, and our fruit becomes evident to all.

"That he might sanctify and cleanse it with the washing of water by the word." – Ephesians 5:26

Water is also employed for cleansing. Similarly, the word of God has the power to purify our spirit and mind.

As believers, our life at every stage depends on the word of God to cleanse us with the truth, empower us with the life within it, and guide us with the light it provides. May God assist us in adhering to His word in every situation of our lives.

Let's Pray

Dear Heavenly Father, thank you for your word. Your word cleanses me daily as it embodies the truth of the Lord Jesus Christ. It encourages and empowers me. I am grateful for the companionship of your word. Please help me rely on your word in every situation of my life. I pray in the name of my Lord and Savior, Jesus Christ. Amen!

DAY 25 - SPIRITUAL GROWTH NEEDS TRUTH TO BE RECEIVED

the word of the truth of the gospel; Which is come unto you, as it is in all the world; and bringeth forth fruit - Colossians 1:5-6

In this verse, we understand that when we hear the word of God, it is only sown in the heart as a seed. But when does it germinate? It germinates when we receive the truth of that word and the grace hidden in that truth. Then our life starts absorbing the nutrition of God's truth and grace, and grows to bring forth the fruit of God's glory in our lives.

For example, if we take a real seed, when we sow it in the ground, it does not immediately sprout. It must receive the work of the ground, water, and sunlight, and then the outer layer must break to absorb the nutrition provided by the ground. Only then does it grow.

Similarly, when we hear that Jesus Christ paid it all and we accept the truth that we are Christians, the truth is that He paid it all and broke the bondage of sin. This means that anything associated with sin—death, guilt, loss, defeat, and diseases—should not rule our lives if we truly receive the truth.

What does it mean to receive the truth? It means believing the word and aligning our actions, behavior, and environment to that truth. Then growth starts in the spirit and one day matures to bring glory to God's name.

Anything that hinders receiving the truth is like rocky or thorny ground. We need to remove those obstacles to fully receive the word of God's truth.
May God help us to understand and prepare ourselves to live up to the potential we have in Christ, Amen.

Let's Pray

Dear loving heavenly Father, thank you for the things you taught today. The word teaches us many of your aspects and characteristics. But because of the advancement of technology, our hearts are not ready to receive the truth as it is. Help us to overcome and submit to thy truth. We pray in the name of our Lord and Savior Jesus Christ, Amen!

DAY 26 - YOUR PRAYERS ARE LIKE SEEDS

prayer of a righteous man availeth much – James 5:16

This verse is common in prayer gatherings. A prayer is like a seed, and answers are the fruit, exceeding our expectations. For seeds to grow, they need good ground.

"The LORD is far from the wicked: but he heareth the prayer of the righteous." - Proverbs 15:29

For prayers to be answered, they must be heard. Only the righteous man's prayer is heard, so we must be righteous. But how? "Even the righteousness of God which is by faith of Jesus Christ unto all and upon all them that believe: for there is no difference: For all have sinned, and come short of the glory of God." - Romans 3:22-23

We are not righteous by deeds but by faith in Jesus. We believe Jesus was born of the Virgin Mary, manifested God's glory, died to redeem us, and rose on the third day. Everything we need is in Christ.

This belief gives us God's righteousness, enabling our prayers to be heard.
"If my people, which are called by my name, shall humble themselves, and pray, and seek my face, and turn from their wicked ways; then will I hear from heaven, and will forgive their sin, and will heal their land." — 2 Chronicles 7:14

Pride, neglecting God, and wickedness hinder our prayers. Before you pray, check your relationship with the Father. Confess and remove anything wrong. Then your prayers will be answered beyond your expectations.

Let's Pray

Dear loving heavenly Father, thank you for today's word. Help me to prepare my life as a good ground of righteousness. Let my prayer seeds could give me abundant fruits beyond my imagination. I pray in the name of my lord and saviour Jesus Christ, Amen.

DAY 27 - HOLY SPIRIT IS LIKE A SEED TO BEAR FRUIT IN YOU

But if the Spirit of him that raised up Jesus from the dead dwell in you - Romans 8:11

If we look at a seed, it appears dried up, lifeless, and dead. But when it is sown in the ground, a miracle happens. A new life emerges from that seed. In the verse we read today, Jesus was dead and buried, but He rose again. It is written, "He that raised up Christ from the dead." So it is God the Father who raised Christ, the Son of God.

Now He tells us that if we have the Spirit of that God who raised Christ from the dead, our dead bodies will be quickened. This does not mean we are dead physically, but that we are dead in the original image of God in which we were created. Without connection with God, we are dead.

When we accept the sacrificial death of Jesus Christ on the cross, we are symbolically putting our hands on the head of the lamb offered as a sin offering. Immediately, our sins are transferred to that lamb, and we are justified as righteous. The Spirit of God, who raised Jesus from the dead, then comes into us to raise us from spiritual death.

Slowly, we begin to understand the love of God, the ways of God, the supernatural abilities of God, and everything about our relationship with Him.
This requires consistent fellowship with the word, which is like water, and a relationship with Jesus Christ as our Lord and Savior. Then the seed of the Holy Spirit will bring forth all the ordained spiritual fruits and enable us with all the ordained spiritual gifts.

To sow the seed of the Holy Spirit, we need to believe in the death, burial, and resurrection of our Lord Jesus Christ.

Let's Pray

Dear Loving heavenly Father, thank you for the gift of Jesus and the Holy Spirit. You made a way in Jesus and you gave me Holy Spirit to lead in that way. Help me to grow more in your Spirit and be a testimony to your glory, Amen!

DAY 28 - HOW ARE YOU SOWING?

he which soweth bountifully shall reap also bountifully – 2 Corinthians 9:6

If a person has a field that can hold a hundred seeds but sows only 10 seeds, the yield will be limited. If they sow all 100 seeds, the fruit yield will be much greater.

Today, God emphasizes the importance of sowing seeds in various aspects of life —meditating on His word, praying, worshiping, fulfilling work duties, caring for family, contributing to God's work, and using our talents. If we approach these sparingly, our harvest will be small.

God has taught us that the seeds we sow determine our harvest. Spending just 5 or 10 minutes meditating on God's word means we only scratch the surface. But when we seek understanding with hunger, God reveals deeper truths, resulting in an abundant harvest.

Likewise, investing time in our children and family, motivating, correcting, teaching, encouraging, and aligning our lives with God's word is like sowing seeds. If we do this sparingly, the harvest will be limited. Generous sowing leads to a bountiful harvest.

"Herein is my Father glorified, that ye bear much fruit." — John 15:8

When our fruit is abundant in areas ordained by God, our Father in heaven is glorified. May God help us identify areas where we need to invest more with a hunger for results and prepare ourselves accordingly.

Let's Pray

Dear loving heavenly Father, I express gratitude for your word. Guide me in investing my time, resources, and talents in the areas ordained by you, so that I may yield the best results in those aspects. Forgive me for not recognizing this truth until now. Assist me in aligning my life with this truth going forward. I pray in the name of Jesus Christ, Amen!

DAY 29 - THE FAITH OF THE SIZE OF THE MUSTARD SEED

If ye have faith as a grain of mustard seed...nothing shall be impossible unto you – Mathew 17:20

Here Jesus compared faith to a mustard seed. To fully understand this, we also refer to Luke 13:19: "It is like a grain of mustard seed, which a man took, and cast into his garden; and it grew, and waxed a great tree; and the fowls of the air lodged in the branches of it."

When we contemplate faith, it often starts with small matters—believing in the healing of less critical ailments, securing a job, or overcoming a debt. Jesus conveys that with a mustard seed-sized faith, like belief in the smallest of things, one can command even a mountain, representing seemingly insurmountable challenges, to be moved, and it will happen. The symbolism of the mountain emphasizes the notion of impossible situations. Therefore, having faith in smaller situations can serve as a foundation for cultivating the ability to believe in the most challenging and seemingly impossible circumstances, and this faith has the power to bring about the desired outcomes.

Genuine faith in small matters generates experiences with God, nurturing our understanding of His capabilities and willingness to act in our lives. This foundation empowers us to face impossible situations with confidence, knowing that Almighty God stands by our side.

May God help us cultivate strong faith, starting with a mustard seed-sized foundation.

Let's Pray

Dear loving heavenly Father, I express gratitude for the lesson on the faith of a mustard seed. Guide me in learning to have faith in the smallest things. Lead me to strengthen my faith, becoming a witness to what you can accomplish in my life. I pray in the name of Jesus Christ, Amen!

DAY 30 - TITHING IS A SEED

Bring ye all the tithes into the storehouse, that there may be meat in mine house, and prove me - Malachi 3:10

The words in this verse are spoken by God Himself. He emphasizes the importance of tithing for believers, attaching a blessing to it, similar to the command to honor one's parents for a long life. Jesus also addressed tithing:

"ye pay tithe and have omitted the weightier matters of the law, judgment, mercy, and faith: these ought ye to have done, and not to leave the other undone." - Matthew 23:23. That means you should continue tithing, but also prioritize law, judgment, mercy, and faith. Without these, tithing is incomplete and cannot bring blessings.

If tithing is a seed, the desired fruit is God's blessings. The relationship between God and you is the ground. The stones or thorns are neglecting God's commandments, judgment, mercy, and faith, while tithing as a mere ritual.

Once we clear these stones or thorns by aligning our lives with God's commandments, fearing His judgment, relying on His mercy, and displaying faith, our relationship with God becomes fertile ground. In this state, when we tithe, God accepts and rewards it with blessings.

1. An overflowing blessing (Malachi 3:10)
2. Protection of our work from the enemy (Malachi 3:11)
3. No loss in our work (Malachi 3:11)
4. Our blessing becomes a testimony to nations (Malachi 3:12)

Let's Pray

Dear loving Heavenly Father, thank You for today's lesson on tithing. Thank You for helping many of us bring our tithes honestly to Your house. Today, there is confusion and false doctrines about tithing. Help us understand the secret of receiving abundant blessings when we tithe honestly and maintain a good relationship with You through Jesus and the Holy Spirit. May our lives be supernatural and a testimony to the world. Thank You for Your wonderful plans for us. I pray in Jesus' name, Amen.

DAY 31 - GOD CAN RESTORE THE SPOILED FRUIT

And I will restore to you the years that the locust hath eaten, the cankerworm, and the caterpiller, and the palmerworm - Joel 2:25,26

Today is the last day of our month-long devotionals on the topic of "the seed." Throughout the month, we've learned various aspects of seeds: their significance in our lives, the right ground for sowing, and factors influencing their growth. Today, God offers us hope by teaching us about the restoration of lost fruit.

"Turn ye even to me with all your heart, and with fasting, and with weeping, and with mourning: And rend your heart, and not your garments, and turn unto the LORD your God" - Joel 2:12-13

God, who gives the seed, enables us to till the ground, sends the rain, and blesses the produce, offers restoration. Applying this to our lives, we may start something, be it a career, ministry, or project with great expectations. Yet, a lack of fellowship with God fills our ground with rocks and thorns, hindering our efforts. These obstacles can ruin our expected results.

But God, in His grace, gives us another chance. We must analyze our beginnings, understand where we went wrong, confess honestly before God, and trust Him. Then, He will open supernatural doors to restore our loss.

For physical and spiritual growth, the ground must be our relationship and fellowship with God through Jesus and the Holy Spirit. With this foundation, we will not experience loss. God takes responsibility for protecting our work, like a father supporting his child's efforts, even more than that.

Let's Pray

Dear loving heavenly Father, thank you for giving us another chance to set right the things and paving a way to restore the lost opportunities. Help us not to be stubborn when your word penetrates into our heart. Thank you for giving me hope to restore the blessings of the work that I initiated. Help me to rely upon you. We pray in the name of Jesus Christ, Amen!

Final Words

As we conclude this month-long journey of daily devotionals, I pray that the seeds of faith sown in your heart will continue to grow and bear fruit. Remember, each step you take in your walk with God, no matter how small, is significant. Continue to seek His presence, meditate on His word, and nurture your relationship with Him. May God bless you abundantly and guide you in all your endeavors.

If you have any prayer requests or would like to share how these devotionals have impacted your life, please share on our social media channels: Facebook (@efjsocial) and Instagram (@efjsocial). Or send your emails to efjsocial@gmail.com. I would love to pray with you and for you.

In Christ,
Bro. Sunil Binkam